A Porthole in the Cosmos : The Next Frontier

Earth King

For permission requests, write to the publisher at
[Publisher's Contact Information]
[Publisher's Email @ pruthviaroundworld@gmail.com].

First Edition.

Published by [Earth King],

ISBN: [978-93-342-3289-9]

Printed in [Across the Globe].

"In loving memory of all those who touched my life and became the never ending stars, whose wisdom and warmth forever echoing in my heart. This is for you all"

"In the vastness of the unknown, we find our greatest truths."
by Earth King

FOREWORD

"Every story begins somewhere — with a thought, a feeling, or perhaps a fleeting moment. In this book, we embark on a journey of discovery and introspection, one that will make us question, reflect, and ultimately understand ourselves a little better. What you are about to read is not just the result of writing, but a manifestation of the experiences, wisdom, and insights that have shaped the author's life.

As you turn each page, you will find yourself immersed in a world that feels familiar yet profoundly new. The words will speak to you in ways you didn't anticipate, tugging at your heart and igniting your mind. This book is a testament to the power of human connection, growth, and the enduring search for meaning.

I invite you to read with an open heart, for what lies within these pages is not just fiction, but a reflection of the truths we all seek."

— [Earth King]

PREFACE

In the quiet spaces between moments, there is a question that lingers—one that doesn't ask for answers, but invites exploration. What lies beyond what we see? Beyond what we know?

*A Porthole in the Cosmos*is not simply a story of space and time, but a reflection of that unspoken curiosity that moves us to wonder. It is an invitation to look at the cosmos, not just as a distant, untouchable expanse, but as a mirror of our own journey. The vastness above us mirrors the depth within us, and in those quiet reflections, we might begin to understand the profound connections that bind us all.

This is not a story of clear resolutions or definitive answers, but rather an exploration—one that leaves space for discovery, for questions, and for moments of silent contemplation.

I offer this story as a window. Whether you peer through it for a moment or linger longer, the choice is yours.

A PORTHOLE IN THE COSMOS: THE NEXT FRONTIER

by Earth King

TABLE OF CONTENTS

CHAPTER 1

THE EVOLUTION OF SPACE EX-PLORATION

HISTORICAL MILESTONES IN SPACE TRAVEL

The journey of space travel is a tapestry woven with historical milestones that have propelled humanity from the confines of our atmosphere to the vast, uncharted territories of the cosmos. It began with the launch of Sputnik 1 in 1957, a simple metallic sphere that marked the dawn of the space age and ignited a fierce competition between nations. This momentous event not only showcased the possibilities of satellite technology but also awakened a collec-tive curiosity about the universe, prompting a series of ambitious missions that would redefine our understanding of space exploration.

As we traversed through the decades, each milestone became a stepping stone towards greater achievements. The Apollo missions, particularly Apollo 11 in 1969, captivated the world as Neil Armstrong took his historic first steps on the lunar surface, a feat that symbolized human ingenuity and determination. These missions were not merely about reaching the moon; they were about pushing the boundaries of what was possible, inspiring generations to dream bigger and reach further into the cosmos, igniting a passion for exploration that still burns brightly today.

The legacy of these historical milestones is evident in our current endeavors, where we stand on the brink of interplanetary exploration. With missions like Mars Rover Perseverance and the upcoming Artemis program aiming to re-turn humans to the moon, we are not just revisiting our past; we are building a future that promises to unlock the mysteries of our solar system. Each ad-vancement is a reminder that the quest for knowledge is relentless, and as we look back at these pivotal moments, we are reminded that the next frontier is not just a destination, but a continuous journey of discovery that beckons us to explore the unknown.

KEY INNOVATIONS IN SPACECRAFT DESIGN

In the realm of spacecraft design, innovation is not merely a goal but a ne-cessity, as we push the boundaries of what is possible. The advent of reusable rocket technology, spearheaded by companies like SpaceX, has revolutionized our approach to space travel, drastically reducing costs and increasing access to the cosmos. Imagine a future where launching a satellite or sending humans to Mars is as routine as boarding a commercial flight; this is the vision that drives engineers and scientists alike. Each successful launch not only marks a milestone in human achievement but also ignites a spark of curiosity that propels us toward the next great leap in exploration.

As we delve deeper into the cosmos, the integration of artificial intelligence into spacecraft design emerges as a game-changer. AI systems are now capable of autonomously navigating spacecraft, making real- time decisions that enhance safety and efficiency during missions. Consider the implications: a spacecraft equipped with advanced AI can analyze vast amounts of data from its surroundings, adapting its course based on unforeseen challenges. This lev-el of adaptability is crucial as we venture into uncharted territories, where hu-man intuition may not be enough to ensure success.

Moreover, the exploration of sustainable energy sources for spacecraft is be-coming increasingly vital. Solar sails, for instance, harness the power of sun-light to propel vehicles through space, offering a glimpse into a future where our explorations leave minimal impact on the cosmos. This innovation not only aligns with our responsibility to protect the universe we explore but also opens up new avenues for long-duration missions. As we embrace these key innovations, we stand on the precipice of a new era in space exploration, one that promises to reshape our understanding of the universe and our place within it.

THE ROLE OF INTERNATIONAL COLLABORA-TION

In the vast expanse of the cosmos, the notion of international collaboration emerges as a beacon of hope and innovation. As we stand on the precipice of a new era in space exploration, it becomes increasingly clear that no single nation possesses the resources or expertise to unravel the mysteries of the uni-verse alone. From the International Space Station to collaborative missions to Mars, the synergy created by pooling knowledge and technology transcends borders, fostering a spirit of unity that is essential for our collective journey into the unknown.

Consider the breathtaking achievements of the Mars rover missions, where engineers and scientists from diverse backgrounds converge to create mar-vels of technology. Each rover, a testament to human ingenuity, is not merely a product of one nation but rather a mosaic of ideas and innovations from around the globe. This collaborative spirit not only accelerates our under-standing of the Martian landscape but also ignites a sense of shared purpose among nations, reminding us that the quest for knowledge is a universal en-deavor, one that binds us together in our pursuit of the stars.

Yet, as we celebrate these milestones, we must also confront the challenges that accompany international collaboration. Political tensions, funding dis-parities, and differing priorities can threaten the harmony necessary for suc-cessful partnerships. However, it is precisely these challenges that compel us to innovate not just technologically, but also diplomatically, crafting frame-works that enable cooperation in the face of adversity. The future of space exploration hinges on our ability to navigate these complexities, ensuring that our shared aspirations remain steadfast as we reach for the cosmos together.

FUTURE MISSIONS ON THE HORIZON

As we gaze into the vast expanse of the cosmos, the horizon of future mis-sions beckons with tantalizing possibilities. The Artemis program, aimed at returning humans to the Moon by the mid-2020s, serves as a launching pad for deeper exploration. With the goal of establishing a sustainable presence on the lunar surface, this initiative not only seeks to unlock the Moon's secrets but also paves the way for the ambitious goal of sending humans to Mars. The excitement is palpable, as each step taken on the Moon will be a giant leap towards understanding our place in the universe.

Yet, the Moon is merely the first chapter in this unfolding saga. NASA's Perse-verance rover, currently traversing the Martian landscape, is not just a robotic explorer; it embodies our hopes for discovering signs of ancient life. As it col-lects samples and analyzes the Martian soil, we stand on the brink of a new era in astrobiology, where the answers to

questions that have haunted humanity for centuries may finally be within reach. This mission, coupled with future crewed missions to Mars, ignites a fire of curiosity and ambition that fuels our desire to push beyond the known limits of our solar system.

Looking even further ahead, the concept of interstellar travel, once relegat-ed to the realm of science fiction, is beginning to take shape in the minds of visionary scientists. Projects like Breakthrough Starshot, which aims to send tiny spacecraft to Alpha Centauri using light sails propelled by powerful lasers, challenge our understanding of physics and technology. These endeavors re-mind us that the universe is not just a destination but a canvas for our imagi-nation, urging us to dream bigger and reach further. As we stand on the brink of these groundbreaking missions, the future of space exploration glimmers with the promise of discovery, urging us to embrace the unknown.

CHAPTER 2

ASTROBIOLOGY: THE SEARCH FOR LIFE BEYOND EARTH

UNDERSTANDING EXTREMOPHILES

In the vast tapestry of life on Earth, extremophiles stand out as the bold pi-oneers of survival, thriving in conditions that would obliterate most known organisms. These remarkable beings, from the scorching depths of hydrother-mal vents to the frigid expanses of Antarctica, challenge our understanding of life's limits.

As we delve into their world, we uncover not just the resilience of life but also the tantalizing possibility that similar organisms could exist on distant planets, where conditions are deemed inhospitable by our current standards. What if the key to finding extraterrestrial life lies in the very ex-tremities that we often overlook?

8

Consider the tardigrade, a minuscule marvel that can withstand the vacuum of space, extreme radiation, and temperatures that would freeze or boil most life forms. These tiny creatures embody the essence of adaptability, and their existence prompts us to rethink the environments that could harbor life be-yond Earth. As we explore the cosmos, the study of extremophiles becomes a beacon of hope, guiding our search for life on planets like Mars or the icy moons of Jupiter and Saturn, where conditions may mirror those found in the most extreme corners of our own planet.

The implications of extremophiles extend beyond mere survival; they are a testament to the potential for life to flourish against all odds. As we harness the knowledge gained from these organisms, we begin to envision a future where humanity can not only survive but thrive in the harshest environments of space.

Each discovery in the realm of extremophiles serves as a reminder that life, in all its forms, is a resilient force, capable of adapting and evolving. This understanding not only fuels our quest for extraterrestrial life but also inspires us to consider our own place within the cosmos, urging us to embrace the unknown as we venture into the next frontier of exploration.

THE SIGNIFICANCE OF EXOPLANETS

In the vast expanse of the universe, exoplanets emerge as beacons of possibility, each one a potential cradle for life. The significance of these distant worlds lies not only in their sheer numbers—thousands have been discovered—but also in the tantalizing diversity they present. From gas giants with swirling storms to rocky planets nestled in the habitable zone of their stars, each exoplanet tells a story of cosmic potential, inviting us to ponder the myriad forms life might take beyond our own blue planet.

As we refine our techniques for detecting and studying exoplanets, the impli-cations for astrobiology grow ever more profound. The discovery of Earth-like planets orbiting sun-like stars ignites a spark of hope, suggesting that we might not be alone in the cosmos. These worlds, with their unique atmospheres

and climates, challenge our understanding of life's resilience and adaptabil-ity, pushing the boundaries of what we consider habitable and urging us to expand our search for extraterrestrial intelligence.

Moreover, the exploration of exoplanets serves as a mirror reflecting our own planet's vulnerabilities and strengths. By studying their atmospheres, compositions, and potential for supporting life, we gain insights into Earth's past, present, and future. This quest for knowledge not only fuels our curiosity but also underscores the urgency of protecting our own fragile ecosystem, re-minding us that in the grand tapestry of the universe, we are but one thread, interwoven with countless others yet to be discovered.

TECHNOLOGIES FOR DETECTING LIFE

In the quest to uncover life beyond our planet, technology stands as our most powerful ally. From the intricate designs of space telescopes that peer into the depths of the cosmos to the sophisticated rovers that traverse alien terrains, each innovation brings us closer to answering the age-old question: Are we alone? The latest advancements in spectroscopy, for instance, allow scientists to analyze the atmospheres of distant exoplanets, searching for chemical sig-natures that might indicate the presence of life. With every new discovery, the boundaries of our understanding expand, igniting a sense of wonder and anticipation about what lies ahead.

Moreover, the development of artificial intelligence is revolutionizing our ap-proach to astrobiology. AI algorithms can sift through vast amounts of data collected from space missions, identifying patterns and anomalies that human researchers might overlook. This synergy between human ingenuity and ma-chine learning not only accelerates our search

for extraterrestrial life but also enhances our ability to interpret the complex signals from the universe. As we harness these cutting-edge technologies, the dream of finding life beyond Earth becomes increasingly tangible, urging us to dream bigger and reach fur-ther into the unknown. Yet, as we stand on the precipice of discovery, we must also grapple with ethical considerations surrounding our explorations. The technologies we deploy in the search for life must be wielded with responsibility, ensuring that we do not inadvertently harm potential ecosystems on other worlds. As we develop tools for detection, we must also cultivate a mindset of stewardship, recognizing that our quest for knowledge is intertwined with the preservation of the cosmic tapestry. In this delicate balance lies the true essence of exploration: a journey not just of discovery, but of understanding our place in the universe.

ETHICAL CONSIDERATIONS IN ASTROBIOLO-GY

As we stand on the precipice of interstellar exploration, the ethical considera-tions in astrobiology become paramount. The potential discovery of extrater-restrial life forces us to confront profound questions: What rights do these be-ings possess? How do we ensure that our quest for knowledge does not lead to their exploitation or destruction? These dilemmas are not merely theoretical; they reflect our own humanity and the responsibilities we bear as stewards of life, both on Earth and beyond.

Moreover, the implications of our actions extend beyond the immediate sci-entific community. The ethical frameworks we establish today will shape the narratives of future generations, influencing how we perceive life in the cos-mos. Should we intervene in the ecosystems of other worlds, or should we adopt a policy of non-interference, akin

to the Prime Directive of science fic-tion lore? The answers to these questions will not only guide our explorations but also define our legacy in the vast tapestry of the universe.

In this light, the field of astrobiology serves as a mirror, reflecting our values and aspirations. As we innovate and push the boundaries of our technolog-ical capabilities, we must also cultivate a deeper understanding of the moral implications of our endeavors. The search for life beyond Earth is not just a scientific pursuit; it is a profound journey into the essence of existence itself, urging us to ponder what it truly means to be alive in a universe teeming with possibilities.

CHAPTER 3

TECHNOLOGICAL ADVANCE-MENTS SHAPING THE COS-MOS

ARTIFICIAL INTELLIGENCE IN SPACE EXPLO-RATION

As we stand on the precipice of a new era in space exploration, artificial intel-ligence emerges as a beacon of hope and innovation. Picture a spacecraft nav-igating the vastness of the cosmos, equipped not just with sensors but with a brain that learns and adapts in real-time. This is not science fiction; it is the reality we are forging. AI systems are now being designed to analyze data from distant planets and stars, making decisions that would take human operators days or even weeks to process. The implications are staggering, as we entrust these intelligent systems to guide us through the uncharted territories of space, revealing secrets that have long eluded us.

Imagine an AI-driven rover traversing the surface of Mars, equipped with the ability to identify geological features and potential signs of life autonomously. This technology is revolutionizing our approach to planetary exploration, allowing us to cover more ground and gather more data than ever before. With each successful mission, these machines not only expand our knowledge but also challenge our understanding of what it means to explore. They serve as a testament to human ingenuity, pushing the boundaries of what is possible and igniting our collective imagination about the future of interstellar travel.

Yet, as we embrace these advancements, we must also confront the ethical dilemmas they present. What happens when we rely on machines to make crucial decisions in the harsh environment of space? The questions loom large: Can we trust AI to prioritize human safety over its programmed ob-jectives? As we venture deeper into the universe, we must ponder the balance between human intuition and artificial intelligence, ensuring that our quest for knowledge does not come at the cost of our humanity. In this thrilling dance between man and machine, the future of space exploration hangs in the balance, beckoning us to engage thoughtfully with the innovations that are shaping our destiny.

ROBOTICS AND AUTOMATION IN SPACE MISSIONS

In the vast expanse of space, where human presence is but a fleeting whisper, robotics and automation have emerged as the vanguard of exploration. These sophisticated machines, equipped with advanced artificial intelligence, are not just tools; they are our eyes, ears, and hands in the cosmos. From the Mars rovers, tirelessly traversing the red planet's rugged terrain, to the autonomous drones mapping the icy surfaces of distant moons, robotics is redefining the boundaries of our reach. As we send these mechanical explorers into the un-known, we are reminded of the delicate dance between technology and human ingenuity, a partnership that propels us toward the next frontier of discovery.

Automation has revolutionized the way we approach space missions, allowing us to conduct complex operations without the constant need for human over-sight. Imagine a spacecraft navigating through the treacherous asteroid belt, making real-time decisions based on its surroundings, all while sending back invaluable data to Earth. This level of autonomy not only enhances mission efficiency but also significantly reduces the risks associated with human error. As we continue to develop these intelligent systems, we inch closer to a future where our robotic counterparts may one day lead the charge into the depths of space, paving the way for human explorers to follow.

Yet, as we embrace the potential of robotics and automation, we must also grapple with the ethical implications of our creations. What does it mean to send machines into the cosmos that can operate independently, making choices in environments where human presence is impossible? The questions linger in the air like stardust, challenging us to reflect on our responsibility as creators. As we stand on the precipice of this new era in space exploration, we must ensure that our technological advancements serve not only our quest for knowledge but also the greater good of humanity, forging a path that honors both innovation and ethical stewardship.

THE IMPACT OF 3D PRINTING IN SPACE

In the vast expanse of space, where resources are scarce and the challenges of survival loom large, 3D printing emerges as a revolutionary beacon of hope. This technology, once confined to the realms of science fiction, is now re-defining the way we approach construction and manufacturing in extrater-restrial environments. Imagine astronauts on Mars, utilizing 3D printers to create everything from tools to habitats, transforming raw materials found on the planet's surface into essential components for survival. This innovation not only reduces the need for costly supplies launched from Earth but also empowers explorers to adapt and thrive in the unforgiving cosmos.

The implications of 3D printing extend beyond mere convenience; they ig-nite a profound shift in our understanding of space colonization. By enabling on-demand production, we can envision a future where entire colonies are built using local materials, fostering sustainability and self-sufficiency. As we venture deeper into the universe, the ability to fabricate parts and structures in real-time becomes a game-changer, allowing us to respond to unforeseen challenges and evolving needs. The potential for innovation is limitless, as en-gineers and scientists collaborate to push the boundaries of what is possible, crafting solutions that were once thought unattainable.

Yet, as we embrace this technological marvel, we must also confront the ethical and logistical dilemmas it presents. What happens when we can print anything we desire in space? How do we regulate the production of potentially harmful materials? These questions linger in the air, challenging us to think critically about the future we are forging among the stars. As we stand on the brink of this new frontier, the impact of 3D printing in space serves as a reminder that our journey into the cosmos is not just about exploration; it is about un-derstanding our place within it and the responsibilities that come with our advancements.

NEXT-GENERATION PROPULSION SYSTEMS

As we stand on the precipice of a new era in space exploration, next-generation propulsion systems emerge as the key to unlocking the vastness of the cos-mos. Traditional chemical rockets, while monumental in their achievements, are now being outpaced by innovative technologies that promise to redefine our journey through space. Concepts like ion propulsion and nuclear thermal engines are not just theoretical musings; they are rapidly becoming practical solutions that could propel humanity to the far reaches of our solar system and beyond. Imagine a spacecraft that can traverse the void with the grace of a comet, harnessing the power of charged particles to achieve unprecedented speeds, while minimizing fuel consumption and maximizing efficiency. This is not just a dream; it is the next frontier of propulsion technology, waiting to be explored.

The allure of next-generation propulsion systems lies not only in their effi-ciency but also in the possibilities they open up for interstellar travel. With advancements in solar sails and electromagnetic propulsion, we are inching closer to the day when humanity can send probes to distant stars, gathering data from worlds that have remained shrouded in mystery for eons. These technologies harness the fundamental forces of nature, transforming sunlight and magnetic fields into the driving forces of our celestial vessels. As we con-template the vast distances that separate us from other star systems, these in-novations ignite a sense of urgency and excitement, compelling us to rethink our place in the universe and our capacity for exploration.

Yet, as we embrace these technological marvels, we must also confront the ethical and logistical challenges they present. The development of advanced propulsion systems raises critical questions: How do we ensure the safety of our crews on long -duration missions? What environmental considerations must we take into account when launching these powerful engines into the cosmos? As we navigate these uncharted waters, we are reminded that the quest for knowledge and exploration is not without its responsibilities. The journey into the stars is as much about understanding ourselves and our im-pact on the universe as it is about the technology that propels us forward. In this delicate balance lies the true essence of our next great adventure.

CHAPTER 4

CHALLENGES OF SPACE EX-PLORATION

NAVIGATING SPACE DEBRIS

As we stand on the precipice of a new era in space exploration, the specter of space debris looms large, casting a shadow over our ambitious aspirations. Each year, thousands of defunct satellites, spent rocket stages, and fragments from collisions orbit our planet, a chaotic ballet of metal and plastic that threatens the very vessels we launch into the cosmos. Navigating this treacherous field requires not only advanced technology but also a profound un-derstanding of the intricate dance of physics and engineering that governs our movements in space. The challenge is not merely to avoid these hazards but to devise innovative strategies that ensure the safety and longevity of our mis-sions, as we venture further into the great unknown.

The stakes are high; a single collision could spell disaster for a mission, oblit-erating years of investment and hard work in an instant. Engineers and scien-tists are now turning their attention to solutions that range from active debris removal systems to the development of 'smart' satellites that can maneuver autonomously to evade potential threats. Imagine a future where spacecraft are equipped with advanced sensors and AI-driven algorithms, capable of pre-dicting and reacting to debris trajectories in real-time. This is not just a dream; it is a necessity for the sustainability of our endeavors in the cosmos, as we seek to preserve the celestial highways for generations to come.

Yet, as we grapple with the challenges of space debris, we must also confront the ethical implications of our actions. The question arises: how do we balance our insatiable thirst for exploration with the responsibility of protecting the space environment? Each launch carries with it the weight of consequence, and as we push the boundaries of our reach, we must remain vigilant stewards of the cosmos. The innovations we create today will not only shape our jour-ney into the stars but will also define our legacy as explorers of the universe, reminding us that with great power comes great responsibility.

THE PSYCHOLOGICAL EFFECTS OF LONG-DU-RATION MISSIONS

As we venture deeper into the cosmos, the psychological effects of long-du-ration missions become a crucial consideration in our exploration endeavors. The isolation of space, coupled with the confinement of spacecraft, can lead to profound psychological stressors that challenge even the most resilient as-tronauts. Imagine the weight of silence, the endless stretch of stars outside your window, and the absence of familiar faces – these elements can warp time and perception, creating a mental landscape as vast and unpredictable as the universe itself.

Studies have shown that astronauts on extended missions often grapple with feelings of loneliness and anxiety, which can escalate into more severe issues such as depression. The closed environment of a spacecraft can amplify these feelings, making it essential to implement robust psychological support sys-tems. Regular communication with loved ones back on Earth, along with structured recreational activities, can serve as lifelines, tethering astronauts to their humanity amidst the vastness of space.

Moreover, the psychological toll of long-duration missions extends beyond individual experiences; it can impact team dynamics and mission success. As we push the boundaries of exploration, understanding these psychological challenges is paramount. Preparing astronauts not just physically, but mentally, ensures that as we reach for the stars, we do so with a well-rounded ap-proach that values the mind as much as the body, paving the way for future generations to explore the cosmos with resilience and fortitude.

FUNDING AND RESOURCE ALLOCATION

In the realm of space exploration, funding and resource allocation emerge as the lifeblood of innovation, fueling the dreams of those who dare to reach for the stars. Governments, private enterprises, and international coalitions vie for limited resources, each with their own vision of what the future of space exploration should entail. The competition is fierce, yet it is this very compe-tition that drives advancements, pushing the boundaries of technology and human capability. As we stand on the precipice of a new era, the question looms: how do we prioritize projects that promise to unravel the mysteries of the cosmos while ensuring sustainable growth and exploration?

Consider the ambitious Mars missions—each one a testament to human in-genuity and the complexities of funding allocation. With budgets stretched thin, agencies must navigate a labyrinth of priorities, balancing immediate sci-entific goals with long-term aspirations of colonization and resource utiliza-tion. The delicate dance of politics, public interest, and scientific merit plays out in boardrooms and legislative halls, where decisions made today will echo through the corridors of time, shaping our presence in the universe. Each dol-lar spent is a vote of confidence in our collective future, a commitment to ex-ploring the uncharted territories that lie beyond our pale blue dot.

As we delve deeper into the cosmos, innovative funding models are emerging, offering a glimmer of hope for ambitious projects that may otherwise languish in obscurity. Crowdfunding campaigns, public-private partnerships, and in-ternational collaborations are redefining how we think about resource alloca-tion in space exploration. These new avenues not only democratize access to funding but also engage a global audience in the quest for knowledge, inviting citizens to become stakeholders in humanity's journey into the unknown. In this interconnected age, the potential for innovation is boundless, and as we harness these resources wisely, we inch closer to the day when the stars may no longer be just a dream, but a destination.

ENVIRONMENTAL CONCERNS OF SPACE TRAVEL

As humanity sets its sights on the stars, the environmental concerns of space travel loom larger than ever. The very act of launching a spacecraft into orbit unleashes a cacophony of pollutants into the atmosphere, from the carbon emissions of rocket fuel to the debris that clutters our skies. Each launch, while a testament to our ingenuity, carries with it the weight of responsibility; we must grapple with the consequences of our ambitions and strive for sustain-able practices that honor both our planet and the cosmos we seek to explore.

Moreover, the quest for extraterrestrial colonization raises profound ques-tions about our ethical obligations to other celestial bodies. The prospect of mining asteroids or establishing bases on Mars invites us to consider the potential for contamination, not just of our own environment but of alien ecosystems that may harbor life. As we advance technologically, we must also cultivate a sense of stewardship, ensuring that our explorations do not lead to irreversible damage to the pristine worlds we encounter.

In this delicate balance between exploration and preservation, innovative so-lutions are emerging. From developing eco-friendly propulsion systems to implementing rigorous planetary protection protocols, the space community is increasingly aware of its role in safeguarding the universe. As we navigate this uncharted territory, it is imperative that we foster a culture of sustainability, one that respects the intricate tapestry of life both on Earth and beyond, en-suring that our journey into the cosmos is not just a quest for knowledge, but a testament to our commitment to protect the wonders of the universe.

CHAPTER 5

PERSONAL JOURNEYS IN SPACE EXPLORATION

INTERVIEWS WITH SPACE PIONEERS

In the realm of space exploration, the voices of pioneers resonate with a unique cadence, each story a thread woven into the vast tapestry of our cosmic jour-ney. During my conversations with these trailblazers, I was struck by their un-wavering passion and the palpable excitement that fuels their quest for knowl-edge. From engineers crafting the next generation of spacecraft to scientists unraveling the mysteries of distant worlds, their insights illuminate the chal-lenges and triumphs of venturing into the unknown. Each interview reveals not just the technical advancements but the human spirit that drives us to explore beyond our earthly confines, igniting a sense of wonder that is both infectious and inspiring.

One such pioneer, a former astronaut turned researcher, shared their trans-formative experience aboard the International Space Station. They spoke of the profound perspective gained from viewing Earth from above, a reminder of our planet's fragility and the interconnectedness of all life. Their reflections on the delicate balance of ecosystems and the urgent need for sustainable ex-ploration echo a sentiment that resonates deeply with our current environ-mental challenges. As they recounted their journey, it became clear that the innovations in technology are not merely tools; they are gateways to a greater understanding of our place in the universe and our responsibility to protect it.

Another interviewee, a visionary in astrobiology, passionately articulated the quest for extraterrestrial life, framing it not just as a scientific endeavor but as a philosophical exploration of what it means to be human. Their enthusiasm for the latest advancements in detecting biosignatures on distant exoplanets was palpable, as they painted a vivid picture of future missions that could redefine our understanding of life itself. This dialogue underscored a critical question: as we push the boundaries of our knowledge, how do we ensure that our ex-ploration is guided by ethics and a respect for the unknown? Each conversa-tion serves as a reminder that the next frontier is not just about technology; it is about the stories we tell and the legacies we leave behind.

PERSONAL ANECDOTES FROM ASTRONAUTS

As I floated weightlessly in the vast expanse of space, the Earth below me trans-formed into a mesmerizing mosaic of blues and greens. Astronauts often de-scribe this moment as a profound awakening, a realization that our planet is but a fragile oasis in the infinite cosmos. The silence of space is deafening, yet it invites introspection, urging us to contemplate our place in the universe and the responsibilities that come with it. Each glance out of the porthole is a reminder that we are all connected, not just to each other, but to the very fabric of existence itself.

One astronaut recounted a moment during a spacewalk when the sun peeked over the horizon, casting a golden glow across the blackness of space. In that fleeting instant, time seemed to suspend, and the enormity of the universe enveloped him. It was a reminder that innovation in space exploration is not merely about technology; it's about the human experience, the emotions that bind us to the stars, and the dreams that propel us forward. This blend of awe and vulnerability fuels the drive to push boundaries and explore the un-known, igniting a passion that transcends the confines of our earthly lives.

The stories shared by astronauts are not just tales of adventure; they are reflec-tions of humanity's innate desire to explore and understand. Each personal anecdote serves as a testament to the innovations that have made these jour-neys possible, from advanced life-support systems to the intricate designs of spacecraft. As we delve into these narratives, we uncover the essence of what it means to be a pioneer in the cosmos—embracing both the triumphs and the challenges, while inspiring future generations to look up and dream of their own journeys among the stars.

THE ROLE OF PUBLIC ENGAGEMENT AND EDUCATION

Public engagement and education are the lifeblood of space exploration, ig-niting a passion for the cosmos in the hearts of individuals from all walks of life. As we stand on the brink of a new era in space travel, it is imperative that we cultivate a sense of wonder and curiosity among the public. Through in-teractive exhibits, community workshops, and educational programs, we can demystify the complexities of space science, transforming abstract concepts into tangible experiences that resonate with people of all ages. Each engagement serves as a stepping stone, fostering a generation of explorers who will carry the torch of discovery into the unknown.

Moreover, the role of social media and digital platforms cannot be understat-ed in this age of information. These tools have the potential to bridge the gap between scientists and the general public, allowing for a two-way dialogue that enriches our understanding of the universe. By sharing real-time updates from missions, behind-the-scenes insights, and personal stories from astronauts, we create a shared narrative that invites everyone to be a part of the journey. This collective engagement not only enhances public interest but also empowers individuals to contribute their voices to the ongoing conversation about our future in space.

As we look to the stars, we must also consider the ethical implications of our explorations. Education plays a crucial role in shaping informed citizens who can navigate the complexities of space policy and environmental stewardship. By instilling a sense of responsibility towards our planet and beyond, we can inspire a new generation to not only dream of exploration but to do so with a mindful approach. In this way, public engagement and education become not just tools for inspiration, but essential components in the sustainable pursuit of knowledge and discovery in the cosmos.

INSPIRING THE NEXT GENERATION OF EX-PLORERS

Inspiring the next generation of explorers is not merely a task; it is a calling that resonates through the ages. Each time a child gazes up at the night sky, their imagination ignites with dreams of distant planets and the possibility of life beyond our own. We must cultivate this curiosity, nurturing it with stories of past explorers and the innovations that have propelled humanity into the cosmos. By sharing tales of triumph and adversity, we can instill a sense of wonder and responsibility in young minds, urging them to become the pio-neers of tomorrow.

The tools of exploration are evolving at an unprecedented pace, and with them, the potential for discovery expands exponentially. From virtual reali-ty simulations that allow students to experience space travel firsthand, to ro-botics that bring distant worlds closer, the innovations in technology serve as both inspiration and education. Schools and institutions must embrace these advancements, integrating them into curricula that encourage critical think-ing and creativity. By doing so, we empower the next generation to not only dream but to innovate, to push the boundaries of what is possible in their quest for knowledge.

As we stand on the brink of a new era in space exploration, it is crucial to en-gage young minds in the conversation about our future in the cosmos. Work-shops, competitions, and community outreach programs can serve as plat-forms for budding explorers to showcase their ideas and collaborate with sea-soned scientists. By fostering an environment where curiosity is celebrated and exploration is encouraged, we can ensure that the legacy of human exploration continues, driven by a passionate new generation eager to unravel the myster-ies of the universe.

CHAPTER 6

THE FUTURE OF HUMANITY IN SPACE

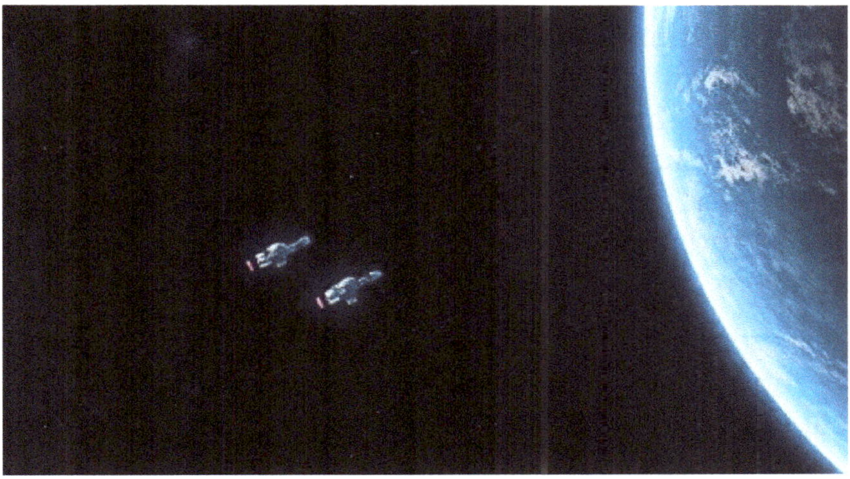

COLONIZATION OF OTHER PLANETS

The dream of colonizing other planets has transitioned from the realm of sci-ence fiction into the tangible aspirations of humanity. As we stand on the precipice of a new era in space exploration, the question looms: can we truly make these distant worlds our new home? With advancements in technology, we are beginning to unravel the complexities of creating sustainable habitats on planets like Mars and beyond, where the harsh environments challenge our ingenuity and resilience.

Imagine stepping onto the red soil of Mars, where every breath must be care-fully calculated, and every resource meticulously managed. The innovations in life support systems and terraforming techniques are not just theoretical; they are being tested in laboratories and simulations on Earth. Yet, as we envi-sion this bold future, we must confront the ethical implications of coloniza-tion—what does it mean to claim a new world, and how do we ensure the preservation of its natural state while forging our path among the stars?

As we embark on this journey, the spirit of exploration ignites a fire within us, reminding us that colonization is not merely about survival, but about thriving in harmony with our new environments. The stories of pioneers who dared to dream of new frontiers echo through the ages, fueling our ambition to push the boundaries of what is possible. In this quest, we must remain vig-ilant stewards of the cosmos, learning from our past as we carve out a future that honors both our adventurous spirit and the delicate balance of the uni-verse.

THE ROLE OF PRIVATE COMPANIES IN SPACE TRAVEL

In the vast expanse of the cosmos, the emergence of private companies has ignited a revolution in space travel, transforming the once-exclusive domain of government agencies into a vibrant arena of innovation and competition. Companies like SpaceX and Blue Origin are not just launching rockets; they are redefining the very essence of what it means to explore space. With each successful mission, they chip away at the barriers that have long held humanity back, making the dream of interstellar travel not just a fantasy, but an attain-able reality. The thrill of watching a Falcon 9 rocket soar into the heavens is a testament to the audacity of human spirit and ingenuity, a reminder that the stars are within our reach if we dare to pursue them.

These private enterprises are not only pushing the boundaries of technology but are also reshaping the economic landscape of space exploration. By foster-ing a culture of innovation, they are driving down costs and increasing accessi-

bility, allowing for a new generation of explorers to embark on their own cos-mic journeys. Imagine a future where space tourism becomes a reality, where families can vacation in low Earth orbit, or where scientists can conduct re-search in microgravity without the constraints of governmental funding. This shift towards privatization is not merely about profit; it's about democratizing access to the universe, inviting everyone to partake in the wonders of space.

Yet, this burgeoning industry also raises critical questions about the future of humanity in space. As we hand over the reins of exploration to private enti-ties, we must ponder the ethical implications of commercializing the cosmos. Who will govern these new frontiers? How will we ensure that exploration is conducted responsibly and sustainably? As we stand on the precipice of this new era, it is imperative that we engage in these discussions, ensuring that as we reach for the stars, we do so with a sense of responsibility and foresight. The role of private companies in space travel is not just about innovation; it's about shaping the legacy of humanity's journey into the unknown.

SPACE TOURISM: A NEW FRONTIER

As humanity stands on the brink of a new era, space tourism emerges as a tan-talizing gateway to the cosmos. Imagine gazing down at our blue planet from the comfort of a spacecraft, the curvature of the Earth framing a breathtaking vista that has remained elusive for centuries. This burgeoning industry, once the realm of science fiction, is now a reality, fueled by the relentless ambition of private companies and visionary entrepreneurs. The thrill of embarking on a journey beyond our atmosphere not only ignites the imagination but also democratizes access to space, inviting a diverse array of explorers to partake in this celestial adventure.

Yet, the rise of space tourism is not without its challenges. The technical hur-dles of launching civilians into orbit safely and sustainably are immense, de-manding innovations in spacecraft design, life support systems, and safety protocols. Moreover, the environmental impact of frequent spaceflights raises critical questions about our responsibility as stewards of both Earth and the cosmos. As we navigate this new frontier, we must balance the excitement of exploration with the ethical considerations that accompany our ventures into the universe.

In this exhilarating dance between exploration and responsibility, space tourism offers a unique opportunity to inspire a new generation of cosmic thinkers. Each voyage into the stars serves as a reminder of our shared hu-manity and the fragile beauty of our home planet. As we look to the future, the question lingers: how will these experiences transform our understanding of our place in the universe? Will they ignite a passion for exploration that transcends borders and cultures, fostering a global community united in the pursuit of knowledge and adventure? The answers lie in the stars, waiting to be discovered by those brave enough to venture forth.

PHILOSOPHICAL QUESTIONS ABOUT OUR PLACE IN THE UNIVERSE

As we gaze into the vast expanse of the cosmos, a profound question aris-es: what is our place in this infinite universe? This inquiry transcends mere curiosity; it beckons us to explore the very essence of existence. Are we mere specks of dust in a boundless void, or do we hold a significant role in the grand tapestry of creation? Each star we observe is a reminder of our own fragility and resilience, igniting a desire to understand not just the universe around us, but also the universe within us.

The advancements in space exploration have sparked a renaissance of philo-sophical thought, urging us to confront our purpose as explorers. Are we des-tined to be conquerors of the cosmos, or should we embrace a more harmo-nious relationship with the celestial bodies we encounter? The innovations that propel our spacecraft into the depths of space also challenge us to recon-sider

our ethical responsibilities.

WITH EACH NEW DISCOVERY, WE

MUST ASK OURSELVES-?

: HOW DO WE BALANCE OUR THIRST FOR KNOWLEDGE WITH THE NEED TO PROTECT THE DELICATE ECOSYSTEMS WE MAY FIND?

In this era of unprecedented exploration, the philosophical questions we face are as crucial as the technological innovations that drive us forward. They compel us to reflect on our collective identity as a species and our shared des-tiny among the stars. As we venture into the unknown, we must not only seek answers but also cultivate a deeper understanding of what it means to be hu-man in a universe that is both magnificent and mysterious. Our journey into space is not just about the stars; it is about the very essence of who we are and who we aspire to become.

In "A Porthole in the Cosmos: The Next Frontier," Earth King takes readers on a thrilling journey through the latest advance-ments in space exploration and technology. This guide is designed for space enthusiasts and explorers alike, offering a suspenseful ex-ploration of the innovations that are shaping our understanding of the universe. From cutting-edge spacecraft designs to ground-breaking research in astrobiology, the book delves into the chal-lenges and triumphs of humanity's quest to explore the cosmos.

With a stream of consciousness style, King weaves together person-al anecdotes, expert insights, and thought-provoking ideas that will ignite the imagination of readers. Each chapter not only highlights the scientific achievements but also poses critical questions about our future in space. This book is a must-read for anyone eager to embark on their own journey into the stars, providing both inspi-ration and practical guidance on how to engage with the ever-ex-panding frontier of the universe.

EPILOGUE

The world moved on, quietly, as it always does. Seasons changed, and with them, the landscape of memories faded, some are fading into shadows, others lingering just out of reach. There were no grand revelations, no dramatic conclusions, only the steady passage of time that continued, indifferent to the stories it carried.

For those who had been touched by the journey, their lives, though subtly altered, found their own rhythms. They moved forward, as they always had, with a quiet understanding that some things are never fully understood, nor are they meant to be.

And so, it remained — a chapter left behind, but not forgotten.

AFTERWORD

As the final words settle, leaving their quiet resonance in the air, I find myself reflecting on the journey that brought *A Porthole in the Cosmos*to life. What began as a mere glimpse into the vastness of space transformed into something more—a meditation on the fragile nature of existence, the ever-expanding boundaries of our understanding, and the unyielding curiosity that drives us toward the unknown.

The cosmos, with its infinite complexities and mysteries, remains an enigmatic canvas—one that we, as human beings, can never fully comprehend. Yet, through stories like these, we venture closer to understanding not only the stars above us but the space within us. It is in our search for meaning, for connection, that we are reminded of the delicate balance between the vast and the intimate.

I invite you, the reader, to carry this journey with you, not as a conclusion but as an invitation. An invitation to look deeper, not just into the cosmos, but into the infinite worlds that exist within each of us.

May you continue to explore, to question, and to wonder?

ACKNOWLEDGEMENT

I am deeply grateful to all whose support, encouragement, and wisdom have guided me throughout this journey. To those who believed in this project and contributed in ways both seen and unseen, your influence has been invaluable.

This book would not have come to life without the inspiration drawn from many, whose stories, ideas, and passions continue to resonate within these pages.

To my readers, thank you for embracing this work with open hearts. It is for you that this story was written.

Have a great beginning!!!

ABOUT THE AUTHOR

Earth King

Earth King is a writer and explorer of the unknown, with a particular passion for the vast expanses of space and the mysteries that lie within it. With a background in Cosmos inspiration rather Enlightenment, Earth King has always been captivated by the interplay between science, philosophy, and the human experience. A Porthole in the Cosmos is his debut novel, a journey into the heart of the unknown, blending the wonder of the universe with the complexity of the human spirit.
When Earth King isn't writing, he can be found "exploring the quiet beauty of nature," "pondering the future of space exploration," etc. Writing A Porthole in the Cosmos has been an incredible journey, one that I never expected to take but am deeply grateful for. This story emerged from my fascination with the vast unknown and the way it mirrors our internal landscapes. Every page is a reflection of the curiosity, wonder, and questions that have guided my own life.
I hope that as you read, you too find something that resonates, something that invites you to look both outward to the stars and inward to the depths of your own thoughts. Thank you for joining me on this adventure.

"The stars above are not the end, but the beginning of something far greater than we imagine"

by Earth King !!!

www.ingramcontent.com/pod-product-compliance
Ingram Content Group UK Ltd.
Pitfield, Milton Keynes, MK11 3LW, UK
UKHW021342190726
13845UKWH00027B/679

9 789334 232899